LITTLE RED
RIDING HOOD

Collect all the books in the series:
The Three Billy Goats Gruff
The Three Bears and Goldilocks
The Ugly Duckling
The Princess and the Frog
The Story of Rumpelstiltskin

First published in Great Britain by HarperCollins Publishers Ltd in 1992
First published in this edition in Picture Lions in 1997
9 10 8
Picture Lions is an imprint of the Children's Division, part of HarperCollins Publishers Ltd,
77-85 Fulham Palace Road, Hammersmith, London W6 8JB.
Text and illustrations copyright © Jonathan Langley 1992
The author/illustrator asserts the moral right to be
identified as the author/illustrator of the work.
ISBN: 0 00 664648 4
Printed and bound in China by Imago

LITTLE RED RIDING HOOD

RETOLD & ILLUSTRATED BY
JONATHAN LANGLEY

PictureLions

An Imprint of HarperCollins*Publishers*

Once upon a time, on the edge of the big wood, there
lived a little girl called Little Red Riding Hood. Her real
name was Brenda but she was always known as Little Red
Riding Hood because this was what her mother called her
when she was a baby. Brenda used to wear a red bonnet
when she went out for a ride in her pram, and she still
wears it now.

One day Little Red Riding Hood was playing out in the sunshine when her mother called her, "I want you to go over to Grandma's house with some groceries. Grandma's not very well and she hasn't been able to get out to the shops."

"Do I have to?" said Little Red Riding Hood with a glum face.

"Yes you do!" said Mum. "Now go and wash your face." Mum packed the groceries into a basket while Little Red Riding Hood did as she was told.

When the basket was ready
Mum looked at Little Red
Riding Hood very seriously,
  "Now, I want you to be
very sensible," she said.
"Go straight through the wood
to Grandma's house. Don't
mess about. Stay on the path
and don't talk to any strangers."

  She kissed Little Red Riding Hood on top of her head,
handed her the basket of groceries, and pushed her out of
the door. Little Red Riding Hood scowled and stomped
off down the path into the wood.

Little Red Riding Hood hadn't been walking far when she heard a rustling in the trees. Then she heard a deep, silky voice calling, "Little girl, little girl, can you spare a minute?"

Little Red Riding Hood was curious and strayed off the path to see where the voice was coming from. It seemed to come from the dark shadows behind the trees. There was a funny smell of old dogs and, for a moment, she thought she saw a tall woolly figure. She remembered what her mum had said but the voice was quite friendly.

"What do you want?" said Little Red Riding Hood boldly.

"Where are you going little girl?" said the voice.

"I'm going to Grandma's house. She's not well and I'm taking her some groceries," said Little Red Riding Hood.

"How kind," said the voice. "What a good girl you must be. And where does your poor grandmother live?"

Little Red Riding Hood smiled angelically and replied in her sweetest voice, "She lives at the far side of the wood, next to the pond."

"What a pleasant place to live," said the soft voice, "but you mustn't keep the old lady waiting. Off you go, dear."

Little Red Riding Hood waved and continued on to Grandma's house.

When Little Red Riding Hood was out of sight the tall woolly figure stepped out of the shadows and smiled a big sharp-toothed smile.

The silky voice belonged to a wolf!

He was hungry and wanted to eat Little Red Riding Hood but he was also clever. He was too near the little girl's house and her mother might hear her scream.

If he took the short cut through the trees, he thought, he
could arrive at Grandma's house before Little Red Riding
Hood, and then he could eat the tasty little girl and her fat
old grandmother. Licking his lips he raced off into the
dark wood.

When the wolf reached Grandma's house he sneaked around the back and peeked in through the kitchen window. Grandma was making a pot of tea. The wolf lifted the latch silently and tip-toed in when Grandma's back was turned. Then, before Grandma could shout, 'tea-bag!' the greedy wolf swallowed her whole.

"Mmm, yum, yum," he said. Then, he hurried to
Grandma's bedroom and searched her drawers until he
found a big pink nightgown and a frilly nightcap.

Quickly the wolf dressed himself in Grandma's clothes
and leapt into bed just as he heard Little Red Riding
Hood approaching the house.

"Grandma, where are you?" shouted Little Red Riding Hood.

"I'm in bed, child," called the wolf in his best 'old lady' voice. "Come right in, the door's not locked."

Little Red Riding Hood opened the back door and stepped into the kitchen. There was a funny smell which was different from Grandma's smell, and the teapot lay broken on the floor.

"Grandma, are you all right?" called Little Red Riding Hood.

"Yes dear, I'm not feeling myself today so I decided to go back to bed. Do come in and see me."

It was dark in Grandma's room because the curtains were drawn. Little Red Riding Hood, still holding the basket of groceries, stood beside the bed. How strange, she thought, there was that funny smell of old dogs again. She looked at the figure under the great heap of bedclothes and frowned.

"Grandma, are you sure you're all right?" said Little Red Riding Hood.

"Of course, my child. I'm just a bit under the weather," said the wolf.

Little Red Riding Hood thought Grandma's voice
sounded strange, but she did have a bad cold. Then she
noticed Grandma's ears.

"Grandma, what big ears you have!"

"All the better to hear you with, my dear," said the wolf.

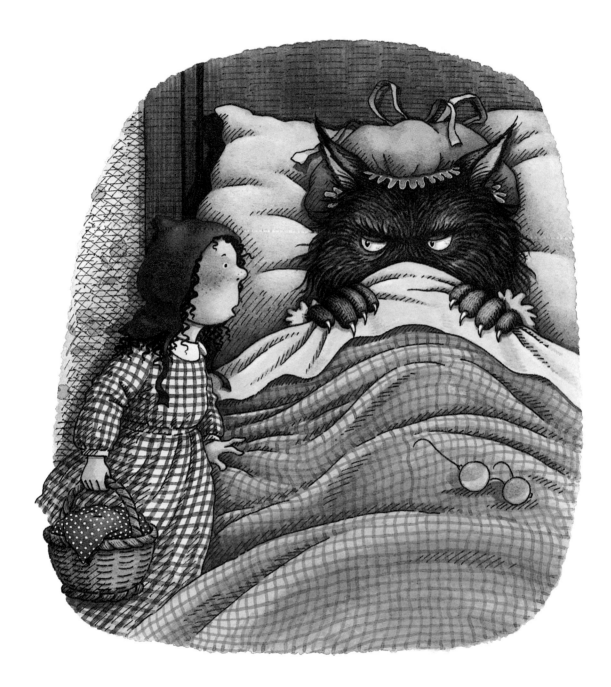

Then Little Red Riding Hood noticed Grandma's
gleaming eyes.

"Grandma, what big eyes you have!"

"All the better to see you with, my dear," said the wolf.

Then, as Little Red Riding Hood's eyes became accustomed to the dim light, she noticed Grandma's pointed nose and shining teeth.

"Grandma, what big teeth you have!"

At this the wolf leapt up and growled, "ALL THE BETTER TO EAT YOU WITH, MY DEAR!"

The wolf's jaws were all around her but, quick as a flash,
Little Red Riding Hood swung the shopping basket and
hit the wolf squarely on the nose. He yelped and fell back.

At that moment the door burst open and there stood Mum with Grandma's frying pan in her hand! She lifted it high above her head, then brought it down with a CLANG! on the wicked wolf's head.

He did not move again.

Little Red Riding Hood ran to her mother who hugged her tight. "Mum, why are you here?" she said.

"I had a funny feeling in my bones," said Mum, "so I decided to come and see how Grandma was for myself. Where is she?"

There was a muffled cry from where the wolf was lying and something was moving in the wolf's tummy!

"Quick, Little Red Riding Hood, get the scissors," said Mum. With a snip, snip, snip, Mum cut open the wolf's tummy and out spilled an angry Grandma. She was shaken but, luckily, not harmed in any way.

"I'm going to teach that wolf a lesson," said Grandma.
"Fetch me my sewing basket Little Red Riding Hood."
   Grandma worked quickly. From under the kitchen sink
she pulled a sack of onions. She stuffed them all into the
wolf's tummy then, with her best embroidery stitches,
sewed up the woolly beast's belly.

Then Grandma, Mum and Little Red Riding Hood together rolled the sleeping wolf across the floor and out of the door. Grandma slammed the door shut.

"Put the kettle on Little Red Riding Hood, what we need now is a cup of tea," said Grandma, who was feeling much better.

When the wolf woke up he felt terrible. His head hurt and his tummy felt as though it was on fire. "Ooooh," he said to himself, "I'll never eat another grandma again."

He never did, and he never talked to strange girls again either.